Duets for Clarinet Students

by

Fred Weber
and
Acton Ostling

MW01131624

To The Teacher

DUETS FOR CLARINET STUDENTS is a collection of popular melodies arranged for two clarinets. All are correlated with Level II of the Belwin "Student Instrumental Course" of instruction. Although intended primarily for training purposes, they can be used equally well for programs or contests.

Contents

The Belwin "STUDENT INSTRUMENTAL COURSE" - A course for individual and class instruction of LIKE instruments, at three levels, for all band instruments.

EACH BOOK IS COMPLETE IN ITSELF BUT ALL BOOKS ARE CORRELATED WITH EACH OTHER

METHOD
"The B♭ Clarinet Student"
For individual
or
class instruction.

ALTHOUGH EACH BOOK CAN BE USED SEPARATELY, IDEALLY, ALL SUPPLEMENTARY BOOKS SHOULD BE USED AS COMPANION BOOKS WITH THE METHOD

STUDIES & MELODIOUS ETUDES	TUNES FOR TECHNIC	B♭ CLARINET SOLOS	DUETS FOR STUDENTS
Supplementary scales, warm-up and technical drills, musicianship studies and melody-like etudes, all carefully correlated with the method.	Technical type melodies, variations, and"famous passages" from musical literature for the development of — technical dexterity.	Four separate correlated Solos, with piano accompaniment, written or arranged by Robert Lowry: Cavelleria Rusticana...*Masagni* The Sioux Song and Dance.................. *Lowry* Valse and Volante...... *Lowry* Song and Prayer from "Hansel and Gretel"..*Humperdinck*	A book of carefully correlated duet arrangements of interesting and familiar melodies without piano accompaniments. Available for: Flute B♭ Clarinet Alto Sax B♭ Cornet Trombone

Melody

Moderato

SCHUMANN

On The Banks Of The Wabash

DRESSER

Theme

MOZART

Dance Of The Spirits

GLUCK

Melodies Of Victor Herbert

HERBERT

Allegro Scherzando

HAYDN

Minuet In G

BEETHOVEN

B.I.C.210

The Whistler And His Dog

PRYOR

Excerpt From Poet And Peasant Overture

VON SUPPE

Canzonetta

DANCLA

Moderately fast - in a singing style

The Stars And Stripes Forever
(Trio)

SOUSA

* = Exchange parts on the repeat.

B.I.C.210

Intermezzo Russe

FRANKE

Surprisin' Haydn

(On a Symphony No. 94 Theme)

HAYDN

(Goodnight
Ladies)

14

Mexican Hat Dance

TRADITIONAL

B.I.C.210

June

TSCHAIKOWSKY

With expression; songlike

Clarinet Polka

TRADITIONAL

D.S. al Fine
[Take last ending]